Bunglebug Stories

The Boogie Bug Beneath the Bed

by Ken Marrs

Illustrations by Mike Motz

To Nicholas and Emma
Keep dreaming
Love, Daddy

Note for Librarians: A cataloguing record for this book is available from Library and Archives Canada at www.collectionscanada.ca/amicus/index-e.html
ISBN 1-4251-0799-0

Printed in Victoria, BC, Canada. Printed on paper with minimum 30% recycled fibre. Trafford's print shop runs on "green energy" from solar, wind and other environmentally-friendly power sources.

TRAFFORD PUBLISHING™
Offices in Canada, USA, Ireland and UK
This book was published *on-demand* in cooperation with Trafford Publishing. On-demand publishing is a unique process and service of making a book available for retail sale to the public taking advantage of on-demand manufacturing and Internet marketing. On-demand publishing includes promotions, retail sales, manufacturing, order fulfilment, accounting and collecting royalties on behalf of the author.

Book sales for North America and international:
Trafford Publishing, 6E–2333 Government St.,
Victoria, BC V8T 4P4 CANADA
phone 250 383 6864 (toll-free 1 888 232 4444)
fax 250 383 6804; email to orders@trafford.com
Book sales in Europe:
Trafford Publishing (UK) Limited, 9 Park End Street, 2nd Floor
Oxford, UK OX1 1HH UNITED KINGDOM
phone 44 (0)1865 722 113 (local rate 0845 230 9601)
facsimile 44 (0)1865 722 868; info.uk@trafford.com
Order online at:
trafford.com/06-2557

10 9 8 7 6 5 4 3 2

Billy Bunglebug was scared,
To sleep without a light.
He often lay awake and stared
Into the dark at night.

He didn't want to fall asleep;
"I have to watch..." he said.
"What if something tries to creep
From underneath my bed?"

"Like what?", asked Papa Bunglebug,
And jumped down from his chair.
He lay down on the bedroom rug;
"Let's see what's under there!"

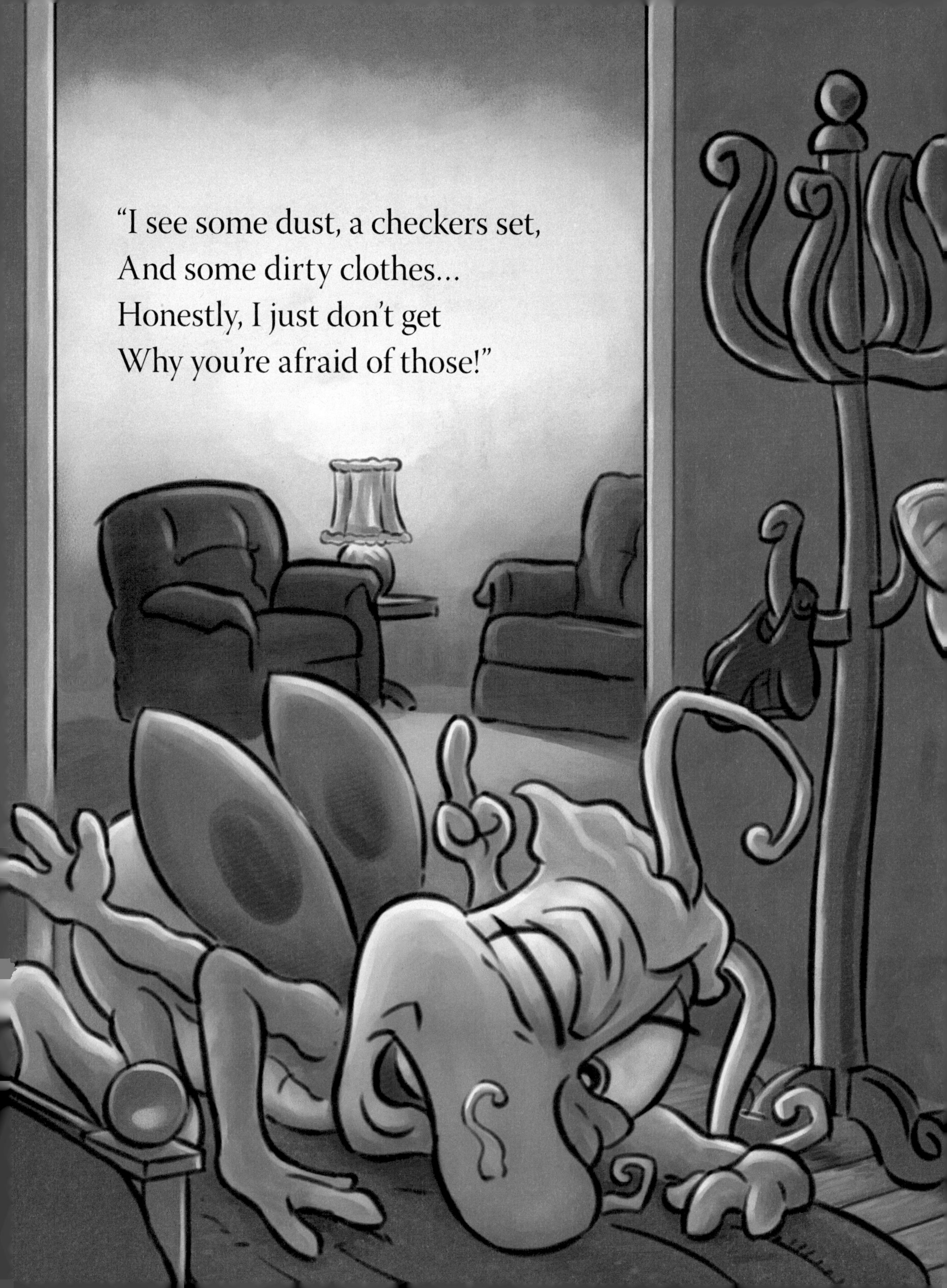

“I see some dust, a checkers set,
And some dirty clothes…
Honestly, I just don’t get
Why you’re afraid of those!”

"But that's not it!" Billy yelled,
And curled up in a ball;
"When it's so dark, I just can't tell
What's in my room at all!"

"And then sometimes I think I might
See something by my door...
But by the time I flick the light,
It's not there anymore!"

When Papa asked; “What do you see?...
A Ghost? The Boogiebug?”
Billy only hugged his knees,
And gave a little shrug.

"There's no such thing as monsters, dear."
Billy's mother said.
"You only see them inside here!"
And tapped him on the head.

Mama said that he could keep
His light on for the night;
But then he found he couldn't sleep,
With everything so bright!

When bedtime once again drew near,
He wondered what to do.
Then Papa whispered in his ear;
"I've got something for you!"

Papa opened up his hand,
Revealing polished rocks.
When Billy didn't understand,
Papa acted shocked.

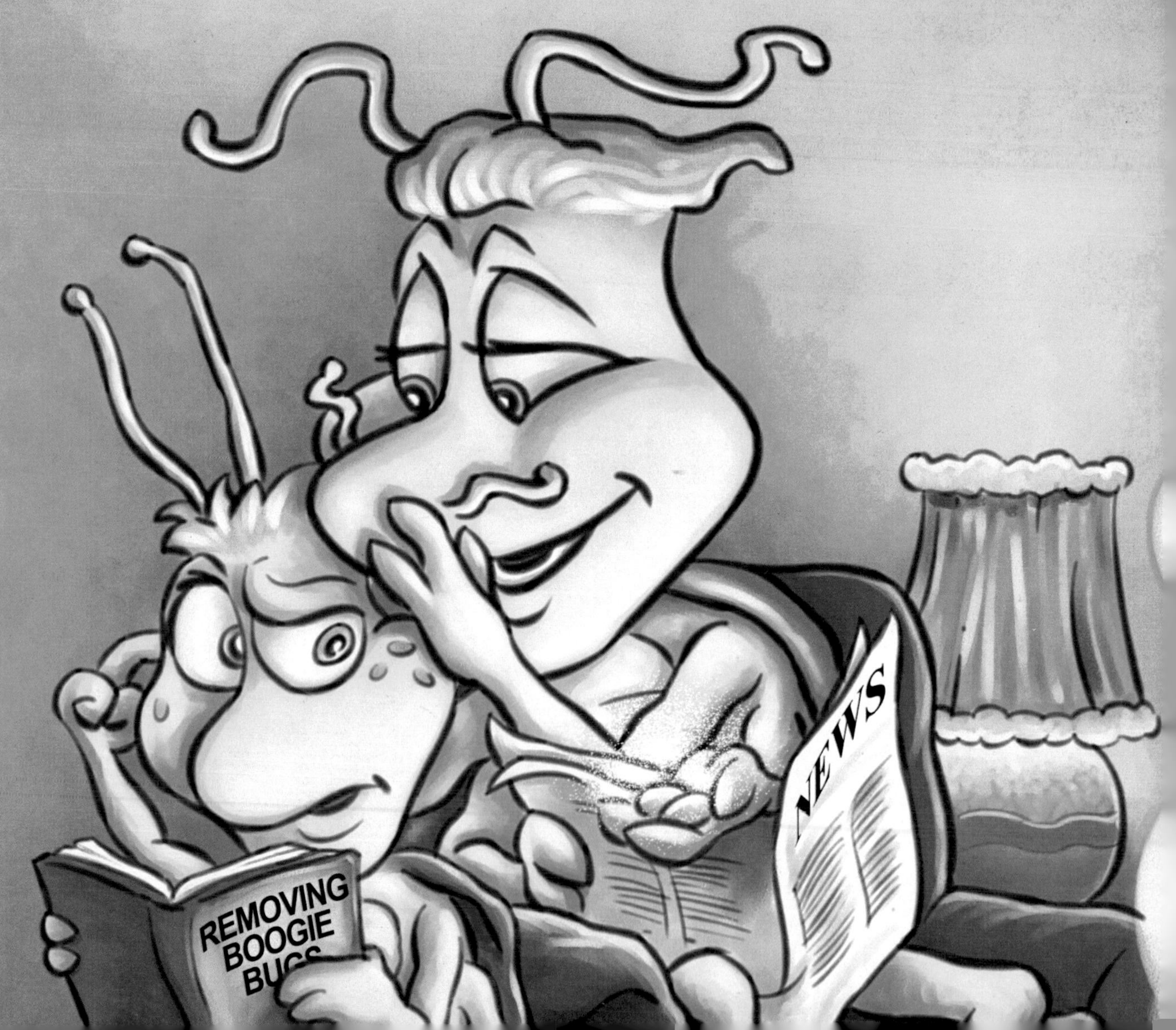

"These are magic dreaming stones!
And Grandbug used to say,
With these you'll never feel alone...
They chase bad dreams away!"

"Now don't be worried anymore",
Said Papa with a grin.
"Once I place these by your door,
The Boogies can't get in!!"

Billy took the wondrous things,
And held them very tight.
No monstrous imaginings
Would bother him that night!

When Billy took the rocks to show
His sister how they shine,
Betty only said, “I know!
Those used to be mine!”

“I used them when I was afraid,
But I have since learned how,
To keep the scary thoughts away,
So I don’t need them now!”

"I think the darkness sets you free;
When all the lights are out,
You choose what you *want* to see,
And what to think about!"

"I think of all my friends at school,
And playing in the park;
I think bedtime's really cool...
I love it in the dark!"

The next night Billy couldn't wait,
To climb into his bed;
This time he would concentrate
On happy thoughts instead!

When Billy Bug was laying down,
And as the day grew dim,
His coatrack became a Clown;
His desk a Jungle-Gym!!

His bed seemed like a Pirate Ship;
His blankets caught the breeze!
He saw a Closet Monkey flip,
From Hanger to Trapeze!

Then as the night grew darker still,
(As if that weren't enough...)
With *no* light from the windowsill,
He just imagined..."Stuff"!

Like...Candy Floss, and Ferris Wheels;
And Santa Claus Parades!
Like Butlers on Banana Peels;
And Ostrich Ice Capades...

When Billy goes to bed each night,
He wonders what he'll find...
He tells his Mom to shut the light,
And opens up his mind!!

The
End